W9-CJS-218

E   R361860
Har   10.95
Harris
The great diamond robbery

DATE DUE			
JUMR 1 '91			
JUN 8 1991			
JUN 2 8 1991			
NOV 9 1991			
MAR 1 8 1992			
NOV 2 7 1992			

BL

GREAT RIVER REGIONAL LIBRARY
St. Cloud, Minnesota   56301

THE GREAT DIAMOND ROBBERY

by Leon Harris

pictures by Joseph Schindelman

ATHENEUM   New York   1985

THE GREAT DIA

MOND ROBBERY

3187689

Library of Congress Cataloging in Publication Data

Harris, Leon A.
The great diamond robbery.

SUMMARY: Maurice the French mouse takes up residence in
an American department store and repays their hospitality
by foiling a diamond robbery.
1. Children's stories, American. [1. Mice—Fiction.
2. Department stores—Fiction. 3. Robbers and
outlaws—Fiction] I. Schindelman, Joseph, ill.
II. Title.
PZ7.H2421Gq 1985 [E] 85-7965
ISBN 0-689-31188-5

Story copyright © 1985 by Leon A. Harris
Illustrations copyright © 1985 by Joseph Schindelman
All rights reserved
Published simultaneously in Canada by
Collier Macmillan Canada, Inc.
Text set by Linoprint Composition, New York City
Printed and bound by South China Printing Company, Hong Kong
Typography by Mary Ahern
First American Edition

For Jane with all my love.

R 361860

In Paris, Maurice the French mouse lives in the palace of the Louvre, a museum full of beautiful objects. When he visits America, he decides to live in a great store because, he explains, "They are the palaces of America, and what's *more* exciting, everything in them is for sale and not only to look at."

There are many big stores in America, but Maurice
decides to live in one called Neiman-Marcus because, "If it's

good enough for kings and queens and millionaires and movie
stars, maybe it's good enough for me."

For weeks, Maurice explores every inch of the enormous store, carefully keeping out of the way of the many people there—some of whom don't like mice.

When he is worn out from exploring but still wants to know what's going on everywhere in the store, Maurice hides

himself in the Security Office. Here there are many television screens, each one showing a different part of the store. But Maurice is especially careful not to be seen by the Chief Security Officer who has an unfriendly-to-mice face.

Maurice's absolutely favorite place is the office of the store's chairman, a man named Richard. Here Maurice always

finds exciting new things from all over the world. The chairman
must decide if they are good enough for the store to sell.

One night Maurice is
secretly sampling some new
Swiss chocolates in Richard's
office when suddenly

he is scooped up by a strong hand! Maurice is afraid he has
been caught by the Security Officer, but it is Richard who is
working late. Instead of harming Maurice or throwing him out of
the store, he asks gently, "How do you like the chocolates?"

The chairman and Maurice become good friends, and
soon the mouse is reporting regularly to Richard about everything
interesting he learns on his tours of the store.

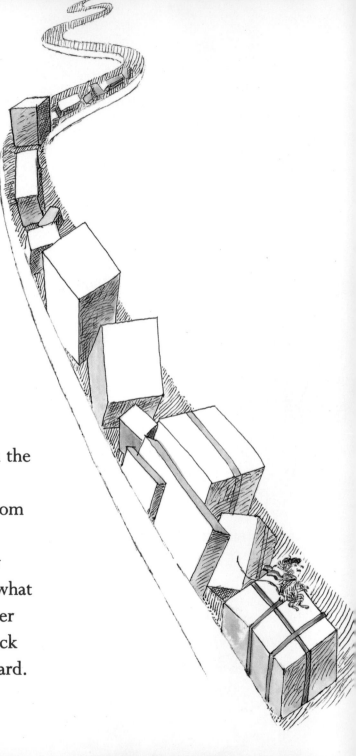

For excitment,
Maurice often slides down the
smooth, steep, spiraling
package chute that goes from
the very top floor to the
sub-basement. All the way
down he shouts, "Wow, what
a toboggan!" And whenever
he discovers a package stuck
in the chute, he tells Richard.

Maurice also reports when the tiny washing machine in the toy department shrinks his beret and scarf;

when the toy stove scorches the cookies he is baking;

when the steering wheel of a battery operated racing car is faulty;

or when any department is not clean and neat. "The Window Display Department is a mess, with sawdust and paint spots everywhere," insists Maurice. "And I'm never going back *there* again — it's too frightening. I saw a snarling Chinese dragon, a screaming, swooping, stuffed owl, and enough swords, daggers, spears, guns, ropes, and axes for a whole lifetime of nightmares!"

Most of the time, however, the store is full of fun and surprises. "This place is really a giant amusement park," he declares, "and someday I'm going to write a song about it."

But one Thursday evening in the
Precious Jewelry Department, Maurice spies
a fierce, fat woman who looks like a mean, manx
cat. She is whispering to an old menacing man
with thick magnifying glasses and the hooded eyes
of an owl.

Maurice sneaks up behind them and
learns they are stealing a two million dollar
diamond necklace. Rather than risk taking it out
of the store immediately, they plan to hide it in the window
display storerooms and come back a week later to pick it up.

The Chief Security Officer is there, but instead
of guarding the jewels, he is gossiping. Maurice watches

in horror as the thieves swiftly, secretly, snatch the
necklace and silently sidle away. Although he is terrified,
Maurice follows them to the Display Department and
sees them hide the diamonds in the mouth of a savage
stuffed tiger.

From the nib of his nose to the tip of his tail, Maurice is shaking with fear. Somehow he summons up all his courage and races up the six floors to Richard's office, so that together they can catch the crooks, but Richard is away!

Although he is petrified at the prospect,
Maurice decides he must tell the Chief Security
Officer what has happened; but before the
mouse can squeak out his story, the officer swings
his club and starts chasing Maurice.

The officer's legs are much longer
than Maurice's, so he can run faster; but
Maurice knows every cranny and corner of the
store better than the officer. Because Maurice is
so small, when he races up the escalator, he can dodge
between the feet of the customers who slow down
the burly, brawny guard.

But when the chase reaches
the Gift Department,
there are too few people
to block the officer, and
Maurice is so panicky he
forgets his usual hideouts.

Suddenly he spies
a group of antique, life-size
porcelain mice. Maurice joins
them and freezes! Can he
stop panting? Can he cease
trembling? Can he keep himself
from sniffling or sneezing
or crying out in
fear as the
scowling
officer
approaches
and surveys
the scene?

Somehow Maurice manages to remain absolutely motionless and silent until the guard leaves to look elsewhere. Then the mouse, cautiously, quietly, slowly, stealthily, sneaks his way to the safety of his secret nest in Richard's office.

When, he worries,
will Richard be back?
What if he is on a trip
around the world and
won't return before the
thieves come back next
Thursday to pick up the
diamonds?

All night long Maurice has the most horrifying
nightmares. In one, he is pursued by the tiger, the thieves, the
owl, the officer, and a giant cat with diamonds for eyes that
follow Maurice like blazing headlights!

But the very next day, Richard returns, and Maurice immediately leads him to the stolen necklace. On the following Thursday, Richard, Maurice, and five brave policemen capture the thieves.

Later, in the chairman's office, over a celebratory supper of Camembert cheese, Coke, and cake, Richard presents Maurice with a pair of tiny roller skates to help him get around the store more easily and faster. "They are also to thank you for your extraordinary courage and help," adds Richard, shaking the mouse's paw.
"Oh, it was nothing, " Maurice squeaks modestly. "What else is a friend for?"

Maurice's Department Store Song

There are people who lengthen a trouser,
And people who shorten skirts
Or who just won't quit until both shoes fit,
So that none of your ten toes hurts.

The customers come in all sizes
From skinnies to mega-plumps,
So fitters are there who, with loving care,
Disguise the bumps and lumps.

There's coffee to blend
And carpet to mend,
Letters to send
And pot plants to tend.
In a store there's really never an end.
In a store there's always more.

There's the doorman who's always smiling,
The cashier who never smiles,
The driver who brings all the things you bought,
No matter how many miles.

The packer who packs the china
So it (almost) never breaks,
The corsetiere who remodels your rear
And the baker who bakes the cakes.

Folks who see that your candles
Arrive for the fête,
On the promised date
And not two days late,
That the elevators elevate
And the escalators escalate.
There are others I've missed.
There's no end to the list.
In a store there's always more.